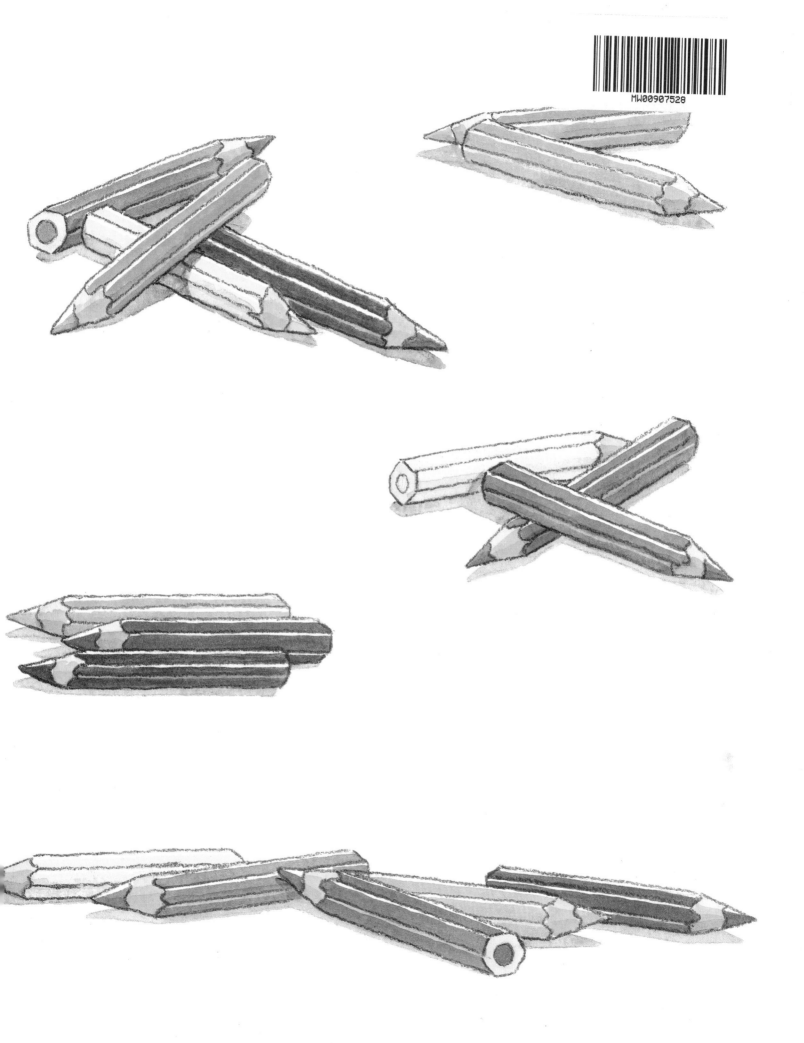

For Tony, Gary and Daniel EM

For Ferghal and Rosie DM

VIKING
Published by the Penguin Group
Viking Penguin, a division of Penguin Books, USA Inc.
375 Hudson Street, New York, New York 10014, U.S.A.
Penguin Books Australia Ltd, Ringwood, Victoria, Australia
Penguin Books Canada Ltd, 2801 John Street, Markham, Ontario, Canada L3R 1B4
Penguin Books (N.Z.) Ltd, 182-190 Wairau Road, Auckland 10, New Zealand

First published in Great Britain by ABC, 1990
First American edition published in 1991

1 3 5 7 9 10 8 6 4 2

Text copyright © Elizabeth MacDonald, 1990
Illustrations © David McTaggart, 1990

All rights reserved

Library of Congress catalog number: 90-50127

ISBN 0-670-83579-X

Printed and bound in Great Britain
by MacLehose & Partners for Imago

John's Picture

STORY BY

Elizabeth MacDonald

ILLUSTRATED BY

David McTaggart

Viking

When John got a new set of colored
pencils he decided he would draw a
house. He drew the walls, the roof,
and the front door with a window
on each side.

Then he drew a little man standing
in front of the house.
Then he put down his pencils and
went to have his supper.

The little man felt lonely. He picked up his
pencils and drew a little woman to be his wife.

The little woman picked up a pencil and drew
a little boy and a little girl.

When the little man saw the children, he made
some extra rooms at the back of the house.

Then the whole family drew a backyard
with flowers to smell and trees to
climb and a swing to swing on.

Then the little boy drew a dog.
The little girl drew a cat.
And the cat drew a mouse to chase.

The little man drew a car.

Then he opened the door and sat in the driver's seat — and the little woman, the little girl, the little boy, the dog, the cat and the mouse, all climbed in after him.

They drove to the store to buy food.

When they got back to the house,
they all went inside to have their supper.

While no one was looking, the little boy drew himself
an extra helping of ice cream and ate it very quickly.

Then the children got ready for bed and
the little man went outside and put the
car away behind the house.

He was standing in front of the house,
thinking of how empty it looked, when John
came back and picked up his pencils.

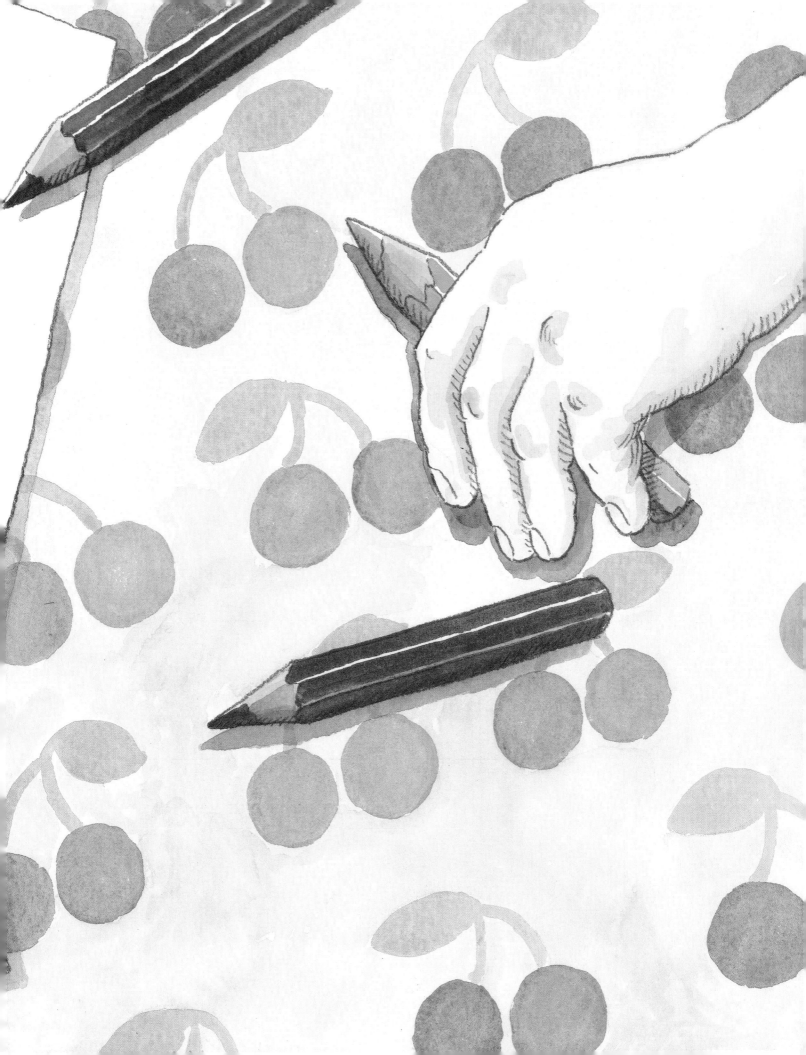

"I think I'll make a garden in front of the house," said John. And, when he had finished, he put down his pencils and went to bed.

The little man wrote a note for the
milkman and fastened it to the door.
Then he went to bed, too.

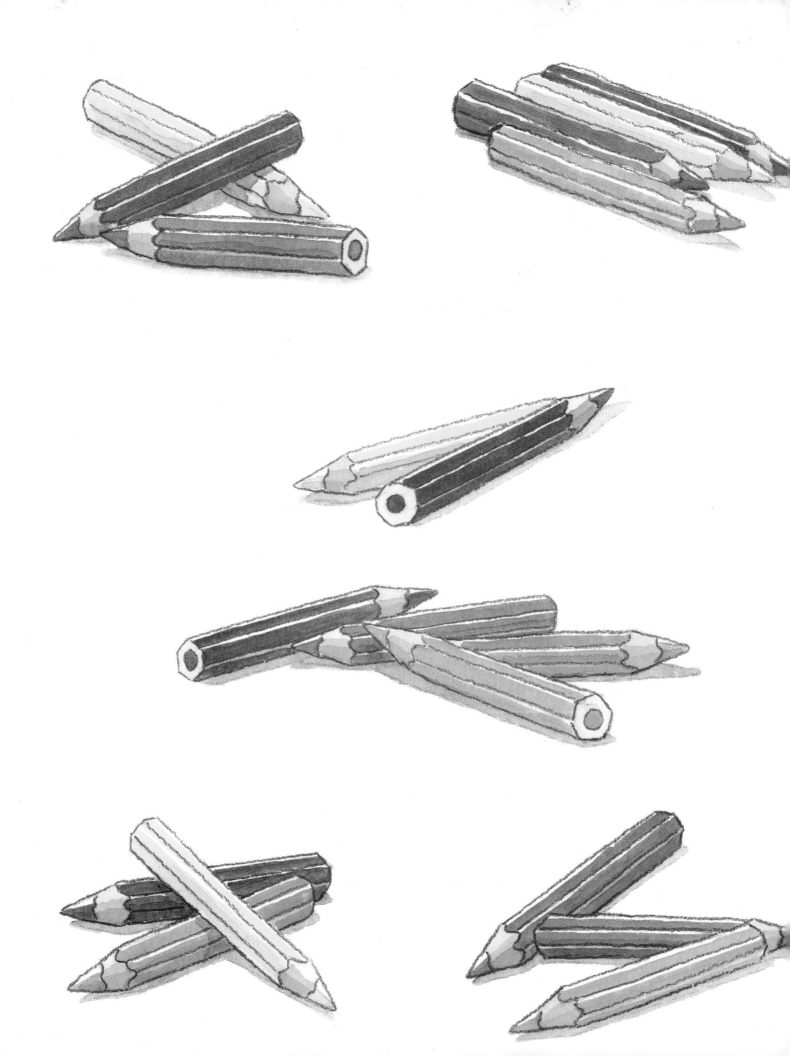